The Evil Mailbox
and the
SUPER BURRITO

By Garry Wagner-Robertson
Illustrated by Connie Wagner

Schiffer
Publishing Ltd

4880 Lower Valley Road • Atglen, PA • 19310

Dedication

This book is dedicated to my family, my friends, and everybody I love, especially my granddad for helping me make the Evil Mailbox.

OTHER SCHIFFER BOOKS ON RELATED SUBJECTS:

A to Z: Pick What You'll Be
Zora & David Aiken Illustrated by David Aiken
ISBN: 9780764337017. $14.99

Beetle Boddiker
Priscilla Cummings. Illustrated by Marcy Dunn Ramsey
ISBN: 9780870336027. $13.95

Don't Be a Schwoe
Manners. Barbara E. Mauzy
ISBN: 9780764334283. $14.99

The Lollipop Monster
Eric T. Krackow.
ISBN: 9780764337734. $16.99

Designed by **IAN ROBERTSON/DANIELLE D. FARMER**
Cover Design by **BRUCE WATERS**
Type set in Kristen ITC/Futura Std

ISBN: 978-0-7643-3856-4
Printed in China

Schiffer Books are available at special discounts for bulk purchases for sales promotions or premiums. Special editions, including personalized covers, corporate imprints, and excerpts can be created in large quantities for special needs. For more information contact the publisher:

Published by Schiffer Publishing Ltd.
4880 Lower Valley Road
Atglen, PA 19310

Phone: (610) 593-1777; Fax: (610) 593-2002
E-mail: Info@schifferbooks.com

For the largest selection of fine reference books on this and related subjects, please visit our website at www.schifferbooks.com

We are always looking for people to write books on new and related subjects. If you have an idea for a book please contact us at the above address.

This book may be purchased from the publisher.
Include $5.00 for shipping.
Please try your bookstore first.
You may write for a free catalog.

In Europe, Schiffer books are distributed by
Bushwood Books
6 Marksbury Ave.
Kew Gardens
Surrey TW9 4JF England

Phone: 44 (0) 20 8392 8585;
Fax: 44 (0) 20 8392 9876
E-mail: info@bushwoodbooks.co.uk
Website: www.bushwoodbooks.co.uk

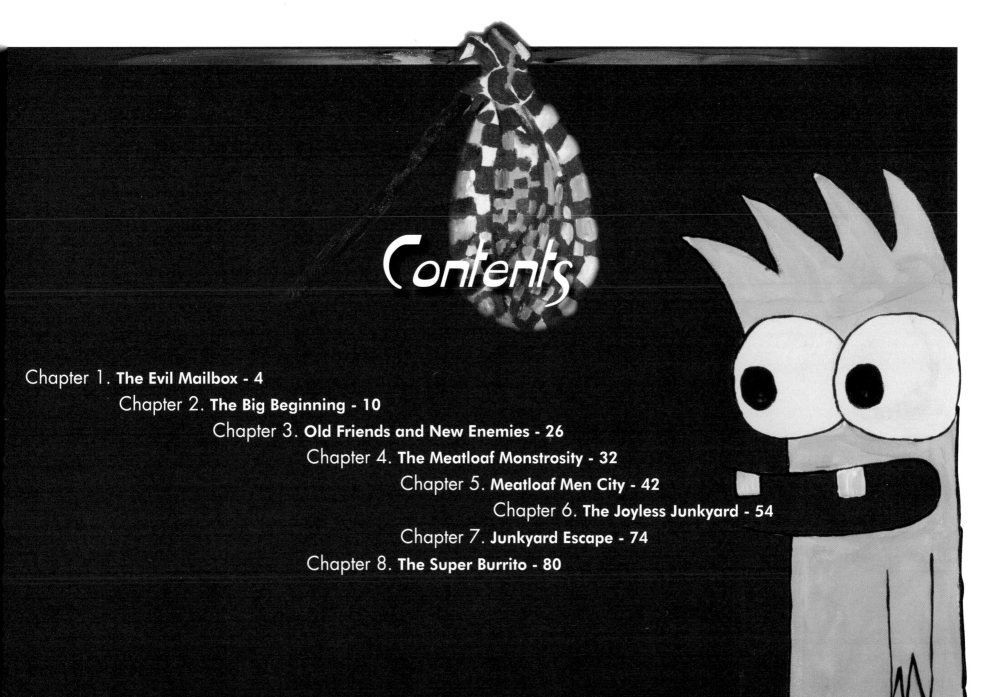

Contents

CHAPTER 1
The Evil Mailbox

The Evil Mailbox was an experiment that was made by Professor I. Gotta G.O. Pee. The old professor was very lonely, so he attempted to make something to be with him.

The only thing he had to spare in the house was an old mailbox, so he grabbed it and ran down to his secret lab.

The professor sat the mailbox in a mutation chamber and set the lever on "Good Friend".

GOOD FRIEND

AMIGO

NUTSO

INSANELY CRAZY

PUREST EVIL

Then, while enjoying a chili dog, he leaned on the lever and it moved down to "insanely crazy". The Mailbox was nearly fully made into a good friend when the mutation went crazy.

7

The machine exploded into dust, and sitting in the rubble was the Evil Mailbox.

9

CHAPTER 2
The Big Beginning

One peaceful evening, the Evil Mailbox was resting on his post (which is a natural instinct for mail boxes) at night when he was awakened by a bright green light.

11

The green light came from a bizarre hovering disk above his owner's house. Then a ray of light covered the house, causing all the food in the house to rise up out of the open windows and into a hole in the strange flying disk.

Then something terrible happened. The Evil Mailbox's last pack of microwave burritos was sucked into the flying disk!

14

The Evil Mailbox wanted to know who thought they had the right to steal his microwave burritos, so he used his owner's fishing rod to crank himself up to the strange ship's portal.

17

When he entered the craft he hid behind some odd tubes of liquid so he could see what he was up against. Then he overheard some strange creatures that were shaped like giant meatloaf.

18

Then the Mailbox realized that he hadn't eaten for three hours and he was very hungry. He thought about the super burrito. He could really use one of those about now. The Evil Mailbox slid down the fishing line and went back to his post.

The next morning, the Evil Mailbox decided to find the super burrito, so he packed a few things and headed out to find it.

As the Evil Mailbox walked through town, he noticed lots of bizarre things happening. When he looked at the TVs on display in the local appliance store, all the TVs were reporting giant meatloaf sightings increasing over the past week. "Local children terrified to go home to dinner...." The Evil Mailbox thought about the meatloaf men that he had seen the previous night.

23

The thought of the meatloaf men sent a shiver down his back and made his stomach growl. By evening the Evil Mailbox had made it to the

other side of town. He could see the peak of the large mountain in the distance and was getting *even* *hungrier* when he came upon a thick forest and a bizarre tree.

CHAPTER 3
Old Friends and New Enemies

The Evil Mailbox stared at the tree, mouth agape. The tree had bark of ketchup, leaves of relish, and apples coated in mashed potatoes so thick the apples looked as if they were white. The Evil Mailbox sat down and took a bite of an apple.

The taste was unbelievably terrible. The Evil Mailbox felt like he was eating an uncooked steak that had been dropped in a toilet. A strange rumbling coming from the ground suddenly interrupted his nightmarish taste experience. The ground shook as if the world was about to collapse. Then, part of the ground exploded into a pile of dirt, from which a peculiar creature sprouted.

You have eaten an apple from the apple tree of the meatloaf men, so now I have to kill you!

The creature had a meatloaf body and head, and the rest looked like an overcooked meatloaf with back legs. The creature had an angry, raspy voice.

Just when the monster was about to strike it was impaled by three arrows. The monster screeched in pain.

BBBBBWWWWAAAAAHHHH!

Then someone yelled to the Evil Mailbox "CATCH!," and a chili pepper whizzed through the air. The Evil Mailbox knew what to do. He ate the flying pepper and waited for the beast to pounce. Then he opened his mouth. The beast was fried to a crisp as the Evil Mailbox shot a blast of raging chili fire straight at it.

Eventually the Evil Mailbox ran out of power, but the creature was already long gone. "Who threw me that pepper?" the Mailbox said to himself. "The only person I told I could do that was..."

CHAPTER 4
The Meatloaf Monstrosity

"SCHMUZZY!!"

yelled the Evil Mailbox. Schmuzzy was a strange creature with huge eyes, yellow hair just about everywhere, and the biggest mouth you'll ever see. The Evil Mailbox and Schmuzzy were old friends, but hadn't seen each other since Schmuzzy went camping in the forest. The Evil Mailbox told Schmuzzy all about his quest to find the super burrito.

The friends set up camp. Schmuzzy fed the Evil Mailbox another chili pepper to get a fire started. They ate hot dogs for dinner and used the tree's ketchup bark and relish leaves, which tasted a lot better than the apples. Then they got a good night's sleep.

They woke to a strange sight. A huge lake had appeared in front of the campsite. The friends stared down at the lake.

It seemed to have no bottom. "Hey!" said the Evil Mailbox, "the lake is changing color!" He was right. The lake switched to a relish green, then a mustard yellow.

37

Then the lake turned a blotchy reddish brown and started to rise. Then arms and a head began to form. The friends were standing at the base of a monstrosity of meatloaf. "Schmuzzy," said the Mailbox.

They decided to fight it. First Schmuzzy threw the Evil Mailbox a chili pepper and he set the monster ablaze.

The monster soon realized it was very powerful when on fire.

Schmuzzy and the Evil Mailbox avoided many powerful lunges by the beast, and when the beast was finally tired they decided to strike back.

Schmuzzy snuck up behind the beast with his sword and hit the behemoth in the back.

Then the Evil Mailbox jumped up and ate the monster's head off.

The monster then collapsed, causing a deafening BOOM.

"Hey, you know something," said Schmuzzy. "What?," said the Evil Mailbox. "We should look for Bob. He is just the guy you'd want for this kind of stuff."

CHAPTER 5
Meatloaf Men City

The beast then crumbled into dust and blew away. The two friends continued to walk through the forest, unaware of what they were about to find.

They trudged through the dense forest, without food or shelter. The Mailbox and Schmuzzy were just about to give up when they came across a magnificent sight.

43

Below them sat a vast city, the most amazing one you'd ever see. The buildings were emerald green, and were connected by passages filled with beautiful plants. Miles in the air, different layers of traffic zoomed around in hovercrafts.

44

45

The Mailbox thought he had gone to heaven until he looked at the people.

"Hey Schmuzzy," said the Mailbox. "Are those meatloaf?"

Then the friends realized where they were. They were in the midst of Meatloaf Men City. Everywhere they looked - animals, people, even the underwear was meatloaf!

46

As the friends walked down the road the meatloaf people gasped in amazement. One wet himself.

Soon they came upon a large building with the words "Invasion Nerds" carved above two big, smelly doors.

47

"ME WANT BURRITO!," screamed the Evil Mailbox as he charged through the doors like an angry bull. Schmuzzy had to sprint to keep up.

49

A long marble hallway stretched away before them. They walked through the long corridors, hoping Bob would be in one. "It would be terrible if Bob got hurt," said Schmuzzy. "Yeah, that would be terrible," said a familiar voice, "just the thought of that gives me gas."

But the Mailbox was prepared. He quickly gobbled down his last chili pepper. Bbbbbwwwwaaaaaaaa!

Every soldier was now a pile of ash. They dashed out of the building and out of the city.

53

CHAPTER 6
The Joyless Junkyard

The three friends walked along in the forest, sometimes losing each other on the trail.

As they walked along, they realized there was less and less forest; the trees and greens were getting smaller and smaller, until soon there was nothing at all.

55

Then they saw it - a giant junk yard appeared before them. There were tons of rust, trash, and rubble. Before them sat mountain high piles of tires, broken cars, and splintered pieces of unknown metal things.

They walked through the junkyard, unaware that they were being watched. They walked for what seemed like hours, until they came to a mountain so large it blocked their path.

58

Just then a car lid popped right off its hinges, and out crawled a horrible thing. It was two times bigger than Schmuzzy, and most strange of all, it was built entirely out of trash. Its head was a steel ball, and its body was made out of two trash cans stacked on top of each other. Its arm was huge, built out of a metal chimney.

And out crawled other things, each larger than the last. Just as the things approached them...

...something fuzzy grabbed the three friends and tugged them under the junk. All was black. Schmuzzy felt cold sweat running down his face. He opened his eyes. "O.K, I must be dead," he thought.

BLACK

He was seeing big fuzzy things.

He looked over and saw his friends; both were asleep.
That sure woke him up.

"Guys...GUYS!" yelled Schmuzzy. "What?"
replied both sleepily. "Am I going crazy, or are
there really a bunch of fuzzballs staring at us?"

"No Schmuzzy, you're not going crazy. I am!!"
said Bob. "And I have stomach issues."

"Bob, you have to be the stupidest thing in all
the world," said Schmuzzy.

"ME LIKE FUZZIES!" shouted the Mailbox.
"I stand corrected," replied Schmuzzy.

"Nope, you guys are not going crazy. You just almost got
gobbled up by the trash zombies" said a voice.

"The trash what?" asked the friends. "The trash zombies. They are nasty things, aren't they? My name's Chuck. I'm the head around here in our hideout. Those zombies will never find us down here."

The three friends looked around. They had crash-landed in a tavern. But this was no ordinary tavern. It was entirely made of trash. There was a stage built out of a broken car, a bar built out of piled tires, and a shoot arcade in a massive, broken RV.

Chuck helped the friends up and sat down at a table. "So, what led you fellows here?" "SUPER BURRITO!" Screamed the Mailbox.

"So that's what you're looking for 'eh? Well I know a good bit about that legend. It is said, long ago, during the time of witches and wizards, there raged a great war

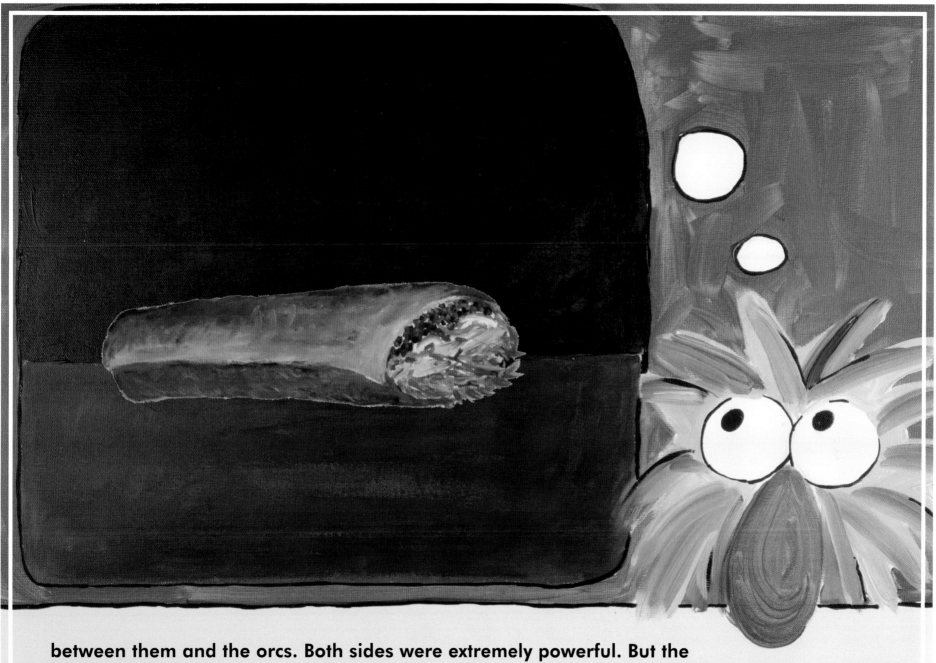

between them and the orcs. Both sides were extremely powerful. But the witches and wizards had something the other didn't. Magic. The witches and wizards needed a

backup plan in case the orcs overpowered them, so they mixed all their magical powers together, wrapped it all in a tortilla, and stuck it in the oven; walla, the super burrito was born! It is said that, if eaten, it will give the eater unlimited power. Enough to destroy a whole universe, or create one," said Chuck dreamily. "The witches and wizards greatly outnumbered the orcs, and the super burrito was never put to use.

"Anyway, you won't make it to the other end of this junkyard without my help." "Well, what you got," asked Schmuzzy.

Chuck led them to a part of the tavern where a curtain hung. "Behold!"

Chuck tore back the curtain to reveal an enormous vehicle. It had huge spiked tiers, a metal dragon head that actually spewed fire, and twin anti-aircraft guns. "I always knew this would come in handy some day," said Chuck.

CHAPTER 7
Junkyard Escape

The trash zombies were still looking for the three friends - what the zombies called "food" - when the ground started to rumble. And out came Chuck, Schmuzzy, Bob, and the Evil Mailbox.

The car shook like crazy as they smashed countless trash zombies. BOOM! BOOM! BOOM! Bob and Schmuzzy blasted at least 300 zombies with the anti-aircraft guns.

BBBBBBBWWWWWWWWAAAAAAAHHHH!

For once, the Evil Mailbox didn't have to eat a chili pepper to burn his enemies. They rode for hours, destroying every single zombie in sight.

76

Soon they came to a whole army of zombies. Piece of cake they all thought. They were wrong.

The trash zombies started to pile on one another. Soon they had assembled themselves into a trash behemoth. It was at least 50 feet tall, had a huge variety of weapons on its body, and the letters C.R.O.G (Crazy Ruler of Garbage) spray-painted onto its metallic head.

The mighty C.R.O.G swung its spiked wrecking ball repeatedly, but never launched a direct hit.

The powerful C.R.O.G got so frustrated it started to spew huge balls of burning metal. One nearly hit its goal.

The huge war raged on, eventually taking them to the end of the junkyard.

The three friends ran for their lives...

CHAPTER 8
The Super Burrito

The three were yet again traveling through the woods. It had been hours since they fled the junkyard. Then, they started to hear a distant rumbling. It was the meatloaf men!

The three friends came to a huge mountain. A big sign said "Welcome To Super Burrito MT".

WELCOME TO SUPER BURRITO MOUNTAIN

They climbed as fast as they could. But soon the mountain started to shake.

It was slowly transforming. Two huge boulders became arms, and the mountain's base became legs. And the head was a massive boulder, with two glowing holes for eyes.

85

87

Suddenly, the beast's head fell to the ground and split in two, and there was...
"The Super Burrito," the Evil Mailbox whispered.

He ran up to the burrito and gobbled it up. At first nothing happened. Then he felt it. Extreme power surged through his veins.

"Wooowwwww," said Schmuzzy, "you're glowing!"

"And you're so pretty," said Bob.

The Evil Mailbox looked down at himself and saw what his friends were looking at. His entire body was glowing with a fiery aura, and he could sense that it was connected to his stomach.

89

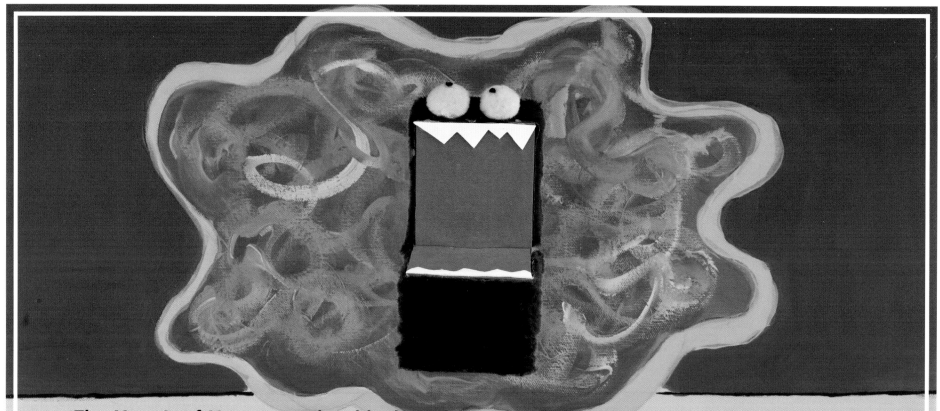

The Meat Loaf Men stopped suddenly and stared at the Evil Mailbox, realizing they were too late, and that he had within him the power of the Super Burrito.

The Evil Mailbox turned to face the Meat Loaf Men. As he did so there was a great rumbling in his stomach, and he opened his mouth as wide as he could...

BWWWWWWWAHHHHHHHHH!
A large blue beam shot from the Evil Mailbox's mouth and struck the center of the Meat Loaf army.

Suddenly a portal opened around them, and they were sucked through into their own dimension.

The Evil Mailbox turned to talk to his two friends, but as he did so the beam coming from his mouth struck them, and another portal opened which carried the three friends away. "I wonder where this goes?" cried the Evil Mailbox, closing his eyes to enjoy the ride.

93

When the Evil Mailbox opened his eyes, he was back on his favorite post in front of his owner's house, and it was a beautiful day.